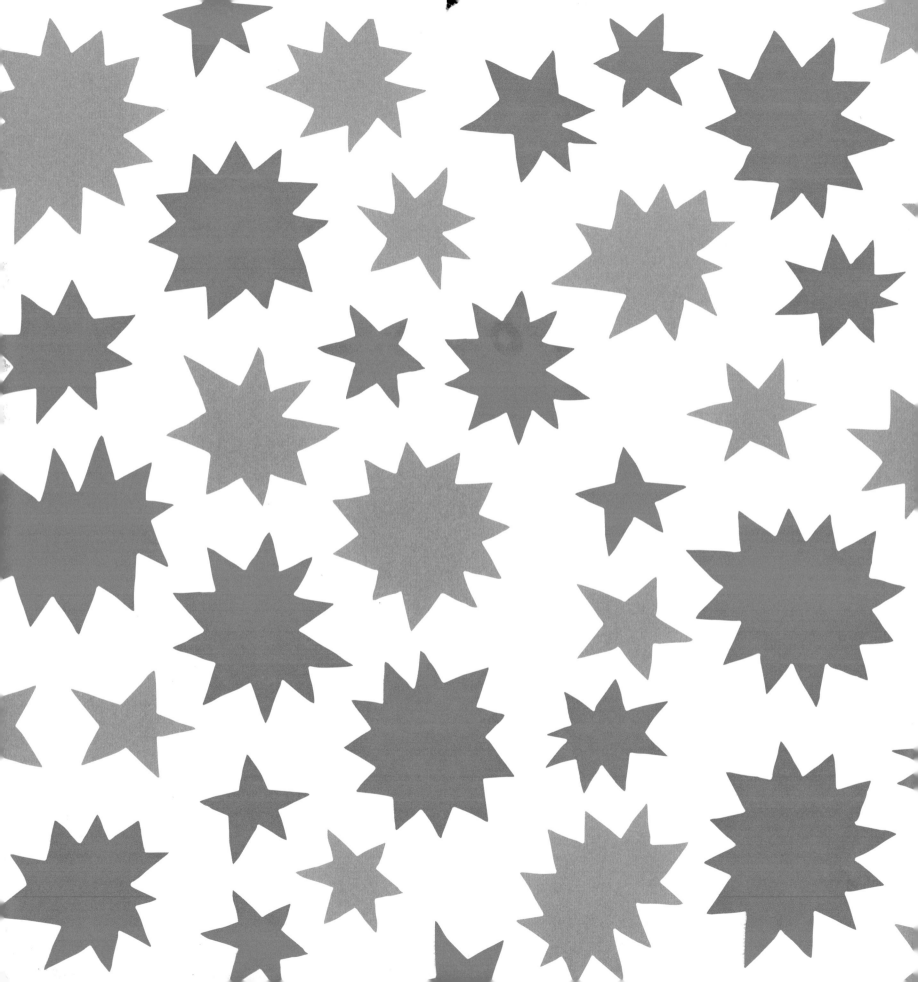

For my girls,
Olive,
Cherry
and **Ivy**

M.C.

Scholastic Children's Books

First published in 2017 by Scholastic Children's Books

Euston House, 24 Eversholt Street, London NW1 1DB

A division of Scholastic Ltd

www.scholastic.co.uk

London   New York   Toronto   Sydney   Auckland   Mexico City   New Delhi   Hong Kong

Text and illustrations © 2017 Matt Carr

HB ISBN 978 1407 17282 8
PB ISBN 978 1407 17281 1

Printed in Malaysia

1 3 5 7 9 10 8 6 4 2

The moral rights of Matt Carr have been asserted.

Papers used by Scholastic Children's Books are made from wood grown in sustainable forests.

SUPERBAT

MATT CARR

SCHOLASTIC

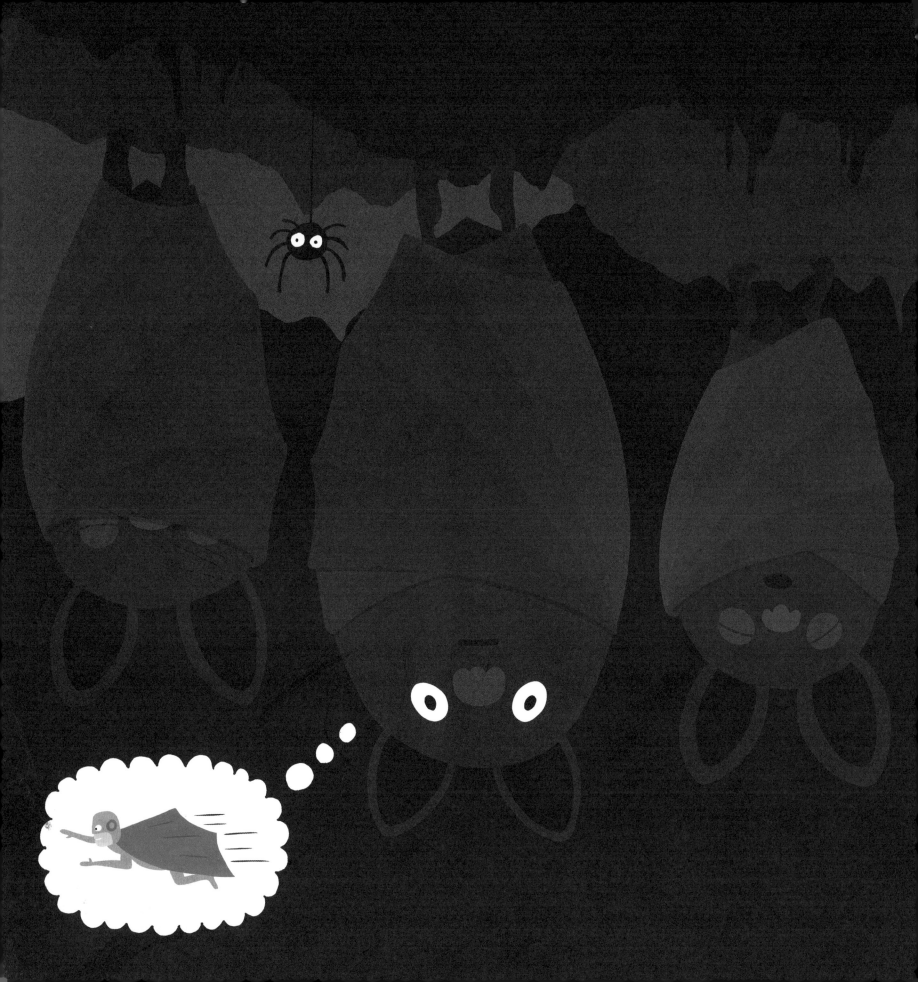

It was the middle of the day and Pat the bat
could not sleep. He was bored of hanging around
like a normal bat. He wanted to be special,
like the superheroes in his favourite comics.

And then it hit him...

POW!

Pat had a great idea and set to work.
It was not easy using Mum's sewing machine,
and his wings kept getting in the way...

but after a couple of hours, his outfit was ready.
Pat became...

SUPER BAT!

When the other bats woke up they were all surprised.
"I'm SUPERBAT!" said Pat.

"Wow," said his friend, Eric, "so what are your superpowers?"
"I have **super hearing,**" boasted Pat.

"SO DO WE!" his friends screeched.
"Good point," muttered Pat.

All the other bats gathered round to see SUPERBAT.

"Can you **lift a car** with your mighty muscles?" asked Eric.

"Or shoot **laserbeams** from your eyes?" added Frida.

"Well no," said Pat, his voice wobbling a bit...

"But I can **FLY!**"
He leapt into the air.

"**WE CAN ALL FLY!**"
the other bats chuckled.
"What ELSE can you do?"

Pat tried to think of another **super-skill.** He felt like every bat in town was staring at him. He was very nervous.

"Er... I have ECHOLOCATION which means I can find my way in the dark."

Pat trudged off home.
His wings drooped.
His ears flopped.
He did not feel special any more.

"I'm just a normal bat in a silly outfit,"
he sighed, trying not to cry.

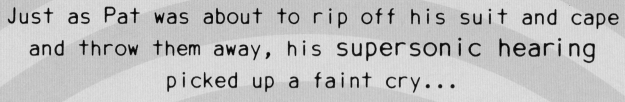

Just as Pat was about to rip off his suit and cape
and throw them away, his supersonic hearing
picked up a faint cry...

On the other side of town,
a **BIG bad cat** had trapped a family of mice.

Pat's wings spread out. His ears perked up. He bravely flew across the city as fast as his little wings would carry him.

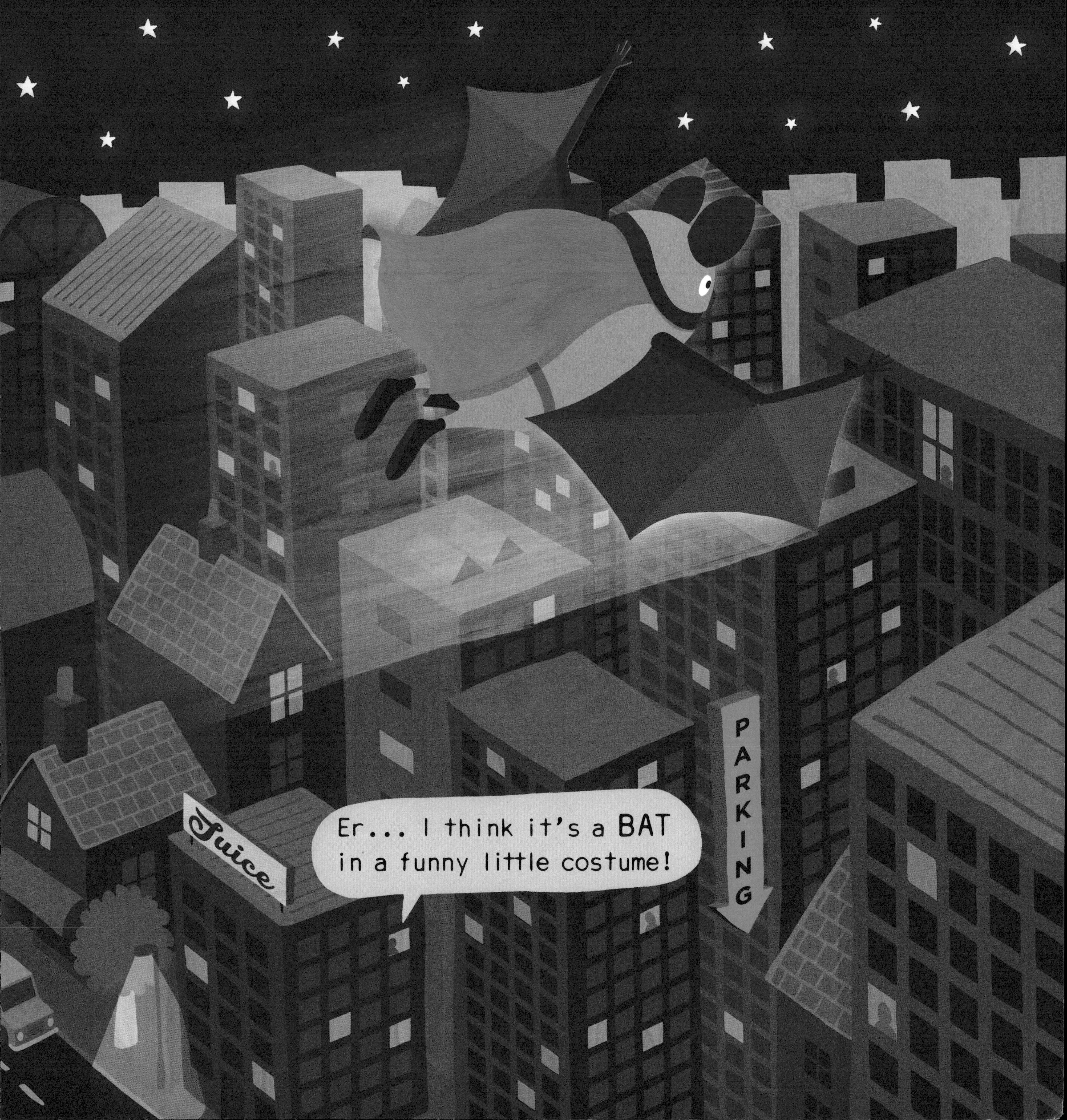
Juice
Er... I think it's a BAT in a funny little costume!
PARKING

The mice were **free!**
"You saved us!" they cried. "Thank you!"
"But who **are** you, oh masked crusader?"

My hero!

And as Pat flew back to the bat cave for a good day's sleep,
with his friends behind him all the way,
he really did feel rather SPECIAL!

BATTY FACTS!

There are over **1,000** types of bat. Some feed on insects, some on fruit or fish. The most famous are VAMPIRE BATS which feed on blood. YUCK!

Bats are **amazing!** But you don't see us often because we are **nocturnal**. That means we only come out at night!

Bats can live to a ripe old age of **twenty!**

We see in the dark using a skill called ECHOLOCATION. We make little noises and wait for the sound to bounce off things in front of us! Our **big ears** then pick up the echo, and we move out of the way!

"That's why all bats are __SUPER!__"